PJ Publishing™

Text and illustration copyright © 2022 Harold Grinspoon Foundation

Published in 2022 by PJ Publishing, an imprint of PJ Library

PJ Publishing creates board books, picture books, chapter books, and graphic novels in multiple languages that represent the diversity of Jewish families today. By sharing Jewish narratives, values, and life events, we help families explore their connections with Jewish life.

For information regarding permissions, please email permissions@hgf.org or contact us at:
PJ Library, a program of the Harold Grinspoon Foundation
67 Hunt Street, Suite 100
Agawam, MA 01001 USA

Library of Congress Control Number: 2021953003

Designed by Michael Grinley

First Edition

10 9 8 7 6 5 4 3 2 1
1122/B1958/A3
Printed in China

HANUKKAH
AT
Monica's

MONICA'S HANUKKAH PARTY

IS TODAY

MAYBE EVEN IN A FEW MINUTES!

SHE IS  EXCITED

THAT SHE CANNOT SIT STILL,

NOT EVEN FOR
ONE MORE SECOND!

SO SHE DOES HER

WILD & CRAZY...

"I - CAN'T

WAIT " DANCE,

UNTIL...

KNOCK KNOCK

THE
FIRST GUEST
ARRIVES!

WHO COULD IT BE?

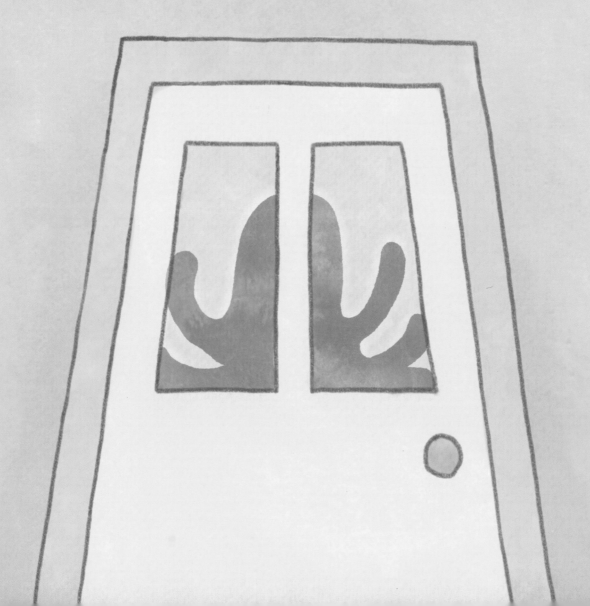

IT'S AN OCTOPUS!
SHE GLIDES INSIDE CARRYING A MENORAH!

IT'S A PIRATE!

HE SWAGGERS IN
WITH A
TREASURE CHEST
FULL OF

GOLD

CHOCOLATE
COINS!

GELT

IT'S A JELLYFISH!

HE WRIGGLES IN WITH YUMMY JELLY DONUTS!

IT'S A DANCER!

HE TWIRLS IN
WITH DREIDELS
TO SPIN!

IT'S A SHINY ROBOT!
HE CLOMPS IN WITH A CAN OF OIL!

IT'S A HANUKKAH MIRACLE!

THE LATKES
ARE MADE AND
EATEN

SONGS
ARE SUNG

MAOZ TZUR YESHUATI...

CHOCOLATE COINS
AND JELLY DONUTS
ARE PASSED AROUND

LATE INTO THE NIGHT.